BRIAN
AND THE
GIANT

BY CHRIS JUDGE AND MARK WICKHAM

THE O'BRIEN PRESS
DUBLIN

On a hot summer's day, a thousand years ago,
a young boy named Brian Boru was busy at work.

Brian loved building clever inventions.
Today he was trying to figure out a way to water the vegetables to make them grow – it had been so long since it rained and the whole village was hungry.

'Something's not right!'
said Brian.

'Let's find out!
Follow that smell!'

'Oh, no!' cried Brian in dismay. 'What's happened to the village? It's all smashed up!'

'I bet it was an earthquake!' said the village chieftain.

'Follow that stink!' bellowed Brian.

It wasn't long before they found some clues.

'Look! Something BIG has gone this way.'

'We need to get down there FAST!'
said Brian.

**When they reached the bottom,
they came across some very unusual trees ...**

'Something's not right!' said Brian,
'These rocks are alive!'

The land was getting stranger and stranger ...
and the smell stronger and stronger ...

'POOOEEE!' said Brian.

'What a stink!'

It started to rain so Brian and his brothers
ran for shelter.

'Quick! Let's head for the cave!'

'Wait a minute, WHAT IS THAT SMELL?'

'It's not a CAVE!' shouted Brian ...

'... it's a NOSE!'

'Smelly giant!' shouted the brothers.

Luckily, Brian had packed a parachute for
each of his brothers.

They landed softly in the forest growing on the giant's shoulders.

'Everyone okay?' asked Brian, as they picked themselves up.

'HOLD TIGHT, let's find out where he goes!'

Soon they were speeding across the land.

'I can see for miles and miles!'
shouted Brian's brother.

'What's that up ahead?'
asked Brian.

'LOOK! He's dammed the river!' said Brian.
'THAT'S where all our water disappeared to!'

'And he's building a bath
out of OUR HOUSES!'

'Hey!' shouted Brian
as loud as he could.

'WHOOO AARRRE YOOOU?'
asked the giant.

'You destroyed our village to make your dam ...

which has slowed the river down to a trickle ...

so now we don't have water for our crops ...

or any food to eat!'

'SOOORRRY...' said the giant.
'I have a plan,' said Brian. 'Come back to our village with us ... but first give us our river back!'

So, with the giant's help, Brian and his brothers built a HUGE shower.

The giant got clean and the vegetables were watered ...

Brian had saved the day and the villagers were happy ...

and the giant smelled GREAT.